DOWN AT THE STATION

Siobhan
Do

WALKER BOOKS
AND SUBSIDIARIES

LONDON · BOSTON · SYDNEY · AUCKLAND

Down at the station,
Early in the morning,
See the little puffer trains
All in a row.
See the engine driver
Pull the little handle …

Choo! Choo! Choo! Choo!
And off they go!

Puffing by the stables,
Past the cows and horses,
Who do they see
In the fields today?

They see the happy farmer
Over in the long grass,
Driving the tractor
And making hay.

Climbing up the steep hill,
Watching clouds above them,
Who do they see
Soaring in the sky?

They see the tiny pilot
Waving as she passes,
Up in her aeroplane,
Flying very high.

Dashing by the forest
And over the river,
Who do they see
At the bottom of the hill?

They see the friendly driver
Handing out the tickets.
The little yellow bus
Is standing still.

Chugging past the harbour,
The seaside and the beaches,
Who do they see
On the waves below?

Going through the town now,
Past the shops and houses,
Who do they see
Working by the road?

They see the busy builder
Pulling on the lever,
And the great big digger
Drops its load.

The journey's nearly over,
Here is the station.
Who do they see,
Giving them a cheer?

Down at the station,
Later in the evening,
See the little puffer trains
All in a row.
"Good-night," says the driver,
As he pats his engine,
"See you in the morning
And off we'll go!"

For Patrick

First published 1999 by Walker Books Ltd
87 Vauxhall Walk, London SE11 5HJ

This edition published 2008

2 4 6 8 10 9 7 5 3 1

Illustrations © 1999 Siobhan Dodds

The moral rights of the illustrator have been asserted.

Printed in China

British Library Cataloguing in Publication Data:
a catalogue record for this book is available from the British Library.

ISBN 978-1-4063-1677-3

www.walkerbooks.co.uk